WE DIDN'T MEAN TO, HONEST!

Robert Swindells

AWARD PUBLICATIONS LIMITED

ISBN 978-1-78270-054-8

Illustrations by Leo Hartas

Text copyright © 1993 Robert Swindells
This edition copyright © 2014 Award Publications Limited

All rights reserved. No part of this publication may be reproduced
or utilized in any form or by any means electronic or mechanical,
including photocopying, recording, or by any information storage and
retrieval system now known or hereafter invented, without the prior
written permission of the publisher and copyright holder.

First published by Scholastic Ltd 1993
This edition published by Award Publications Limited 2014

Published by Award Publications Limited,
The Old Riding School, The Welbeck Estate,
Worksop, Nottinghamshire, S80 3LR

www.awardpublications.co.uk

14 1

Printed in the United Kingdom

CONTENTS

WE DIDN'T MEAN TO, HONEST!

CHAPTER 1

FILL IN FROGLET POND?

The Denton girls looked glum as they left their parents' farm and took the path into Weeping Wood. Jillo was nine and Titch was seven and they were both angry and upset.

"It shouldn't be allowed!" snapped Titch. "Nobody's got the right to fill in Froglet Pond."

Her sister pulled a face. "Mr Kilchaffinch has," she said. "It's on his land." Reuben Kilchaffinch was their closest neighbour – a sour old farmer who disliked children and seldom spoke to anyone in Lenton.

"But why can't he turn the old barn into a house without filling in the pond?"

Jillo shrugged. "I dunno, Titch. I suppose he could if he wanted to, but you know what he's like. He's always hated kids visiting the pond. I suppose he wants to make sure we all stay away when the house is ready and his miserable son moves in with Prunella, or whatever they call her."

"Well, I hope the place falls down on them, that's all!" spat Titch.

When the two girls reached the clearing where the caravan stood, they found Mickey sitting on the step with his breakfast while Raider ate his at the table. Raider was Mickey's dog, but he liked to pretend to be human.

"Hi, girls!" cried Mickey. "Why the long faces? It's the holidays, for goodness' sake."

"Your face'll be long," Titch told him, "when you hear what's happening." They told him about Reuben Kilchaffinch and Froglet Pond. When they'd finished he sighed.

"It's bad all right," he said. "Those poor frogs. Where will they spawn when Froglet Pond's filled in?"

"And the sticklebacks," reminded Titch. "And the water beetles. What about them?"

"Yes, and don't forget the dragonflies," put in Jillo.

Mickey nodded thoughtfully. "They're all going to die," he murmured.

"Unless…"

Titch glanced at him. "Unless what?"

Before Mickey could answer, there was a warning yap from Raider and a boy appeared from under the trees. "Shut up Raider," growled Mickey. "It's only Shaz." He waved. "Hi, Shaz!"

Shaz approached, grinning. "What we doing today, then?"

"It's funny you should ask that," said Mickey. "The girls have just told me something very serious – so serious, I think it's a job for The Outfit." The Outfit was the name they'd chosen for their gang. Raider was a member of The Outfit, of course. Briefly, Mickey told Shaz about the pond.

"But what can we do?" cried Shaz. "I mean, how can four kids and a dog stop that miserable old so-and-so filling in his own pond?"

Mickey smiled. "We're The Outfit. There's nothing we can't do if we put our minds to it, is there?"

"No, there isn't," growled Jillo. "So watch out, Reuben Kilchaffinch!"

"The oath!" whooped Titch. "Let's do the oath." She wasn't looking glum any more. The four held hands in a circle round Raider and chanted:

> "Faithful, fearless, full of fun,
> Winter, summer, rain or sun,
> One for five and five for one –
> THE OUTFIT!"

On the last word they leapt high in the air and Raider barked. The Outfit was ready for action again.

CHAPTER 2

A WELL-KNOWN FACT

"So," Mickey gazed at his companions, "what's the first step?" They were seated round the table in the caravan's snug room. Raider was lying in the doorway, looking out. There were no grown-ups about – Mickey's dad was away most of the time and his mum had left when he was small.

"The first step is to make a plan," said Jillo. "You can't do anything properly if you haven't got a plan."

Shaz nodded. "That's right, Jillo. Have you thought of anything?"

"I've got a suggestion, yes."

"Let's hear it, then."

"Well," said Jillo, "I'm thinking about Prunella."

Shaz grinned. "The woman who's going to

marry our charming librarian?"

Jillo nodded. "Yes, poor thing." The librarian in question was Kenneth Kilchaffinch, son and only child of Reuben Kilchaffinch. He was in charge of the children's section at the village library, and Jillo believed it was his fault kids in Lenton didn't read much.

"Ugh!" Titch pulled a face. "Fancy marrying him. I'd rather marry a brontosaurus."

"You probably will," said her sister. "Anyway, what I was thinking was this." She paused for dramatic effect. The others waited. "Prunella's a city girl, right? She hates the country."

Mickey's eyebrows went up. "Does she?"

"Oh, yes. It's a well-known fact. Mum says the whole village knows Reuben's only converting the barn as a sort of bribe to get Prunella to come and live here."

"I didn't know that," said Mickey. "But anyway, what about it, Jillo?"

Jillo smiled. "What if Prunella decided she couldn't possibly live in Lenton – not even in a luxury barn conversion? There'd be no point converting the barn then, and no point in filling in the pond."

Shaz looked at her. "You mean we should—?"

Jillo nodded. "I mean we should work on Prunella. Convince her she was right the first time – the country's a horrible place to live."

"How do we do that?" cried Mickey.

"Oh, I can think of ways," Jillo smiled mysteriously. "Lots of ways."

"Yeah – such as what?"

"Well, slugs for a start."

Jillo nodded. "City people can't stand creepy-crawlies. That's why they don't like the country. So the best way with Prunella is to start with slugs and work up."

Mickey shook his head. "You've lost me, Jillo."

"Me too," murmured Shaz.

"I think you'd better start at the beginning," said Titch. "Tell us what you mean."

CHAPTER 3

HORRID LITTLE GIRL

It was half-past eleven the next morning when Titch walked into the library carrying something in a brown paper bag. Kenneth Kilchaffinch eyed her suspiciously from behind his counter. He was a thin young man with round glasses and a ginger moustache.

"Just a minute!" he rapped. "What have you got there?"

"Jam," said Titch. "Strawberry. It's for my mum."

"Hmm. Well don't go smearing it on my books, or I'll push your fingers up your nose and pull your eyeballs down. And no talking either, d'you hear?"

Titch looked all round. The children's section was deserted as usual. "There's nobody to talk to," she chirped.

14

"Good," snapped Kilchaffinch. "That's just the way I like it – no horrible little hooligans putting their grubby paws on my stock, making the shelves untidy." He leaned over the counter to glare at Titch's trainers. "Did you wipe your feet on the mat?"

"Yes, Mr Kilchaffinch."

"Right. You can come in, but don't touch anything."

Titch had no intention of touching anything. She wasn't here for books. She was on a crucial mission for The Outfit. She was here because it was Tuesday, the day Prunella always drove from the city to visit her boyfriend. She'd arrive at the library at a quarter to twelve, and at twelve o'clock Kenneth would close the children's section and he and Prunella would go off to lunch at the Fox and Pheasant.

Titch loitered behind the racks of books, pretending she was looking for something. She knew Kenneth wouldn't offer help – he'd leave a kid searching the shelves all day before he'd stir from his place behind the counter. He hated kids as much as his miserable father did, and had only left the farm because he was scared of cows. The only time he was ever nice to a child was when Prunella was watching him.

She arrived at the usual time. Titch spied on the couple through a gap in the books, screwing up her nose when Prunella kissed Kenneth on the mouth. How can she do that? She asked herself.

Having received his kiss, the librarian left the counter and approached the shelves with a yucky smile on his face. "Can I help you, my dear?" he called. "Having difficulty finding what we want, are we?"

Titch grabbed the nearest book and held it up as Kenneth appeared round the fixture. "It's okay, thanks, Mr Kilchaffinch," she smiled. "I've found it."

"Splendid," simpered the librarian, rubbing his hands together. "What a clever girl, and so pretty." He turned and called to Prunella, "Don't you think she's pretty, my love?"

"What?" Prunella stopped buffing her nails on her sleeve and looked up. "Oh, yes – very pretty, dearest. Are you nearly ready?"

"I just have to…" Kenneth indicated the washroom.

Prunella sighed. It was always the same. She always had to wait five minutes while the vain creature combed his moustache. Titch grinned. It was what she'd counted on.

As the washroom door closed behind Kenneth Kilchaffinch, Titch sidled up to Prunella, clutching the brown paper bag. "D'you want to see my slugs?" she asked.

"N-no, dear, I don't think I do," murmured Prunella, but Titch shoved her hand in the bag and produced a slimy-looking jam jar with nine fat slugs in it. Prunella recoiled with a small cry of disgust, but Titch thrust the jar towards her.

"They won't hurt you, missus. My mum sent me to get 'em. They're good 'uns, aren't they?"

"Yes, dear, I suppose they are." Prunella flapped her pale thin hands at the jar. "Would you mind putting them away now – I'm about to eat lunch."

"That's what my mum wants 'em for," beamed Titch. "Lunch."

Prunella paled. "D'you mean to say your mother—?"

"Eats 'em?" Titch nodded vigorously. "Oh, arr. One in the stew and one in the pie. Everyone in Lenton does it, missus. Good for the rheumatics, see?"

Prunella gulped. "Everyone does it, you say?

Everyone?"

"Oh, arr. Yon field by Froglet Pond's fair heavin' with 'em, see? And there's no sense lettin' free grub go to waste, is there? Look, I gotta go now – my mum'll be waitin' for these – but I can spare you one if you want a little appetizer before your lunch, like." She plunged her hand into the jar and groped around.

Prunella covered her mouth with her fingers and shrieked. "Go away! Go on – get away from me, you horrid little girl!"

The washroom door swung open. Titch fled.

CHAPTER 4

ROUND ONE TO US

"So, how did it go?" asked Mickey. It was two o'clock. Titch and Jillo had rejoined Raider and the boys in the caravan.

"It was brilliant!" cried Jillo. "Titch must've done a terrific job – Prunella's appetite was completely ruined."

"How d'you know?" asked Shaz.

"I hung about outside the library, and when Kenneth and Prunella came out I followed them. He was heading for the Fox and Pheasant as usual, but Prunella told him she'd never eat there again. She actually looked quite ill, poor thing. Anyway, Kenneth started arguing and Prunella wouldn't tell him why she'd gone off the place and they ended up having this terrific row, right outside the pub. They were so busy screaming at each other they never noticed me.

In the end, Prunella flounced off and left him standing there, red in the face." Jillo shrugged, grinning. "Then I joined Titch at the bus shelter and we went home for lunch."

"And what was it, Jillo?" chuckled Shaz. "Stewed slugs?" Everybody laughed except Raider, who wagged his tail.

"Round one to us, I think," said Mickey. "Well done, Titch."

Titch shrugged. "It was easy."

"So what's next?" asked Jillo.

Shaz grinned. "I've got an idea."

Mickey looked at him. "Go on, then."

"Murder in the old barn," said Shaz.

"Hey, just a minute!" cried Jillo. "I don't mind playing a few tricks and telling a couple of harmless fibs if it'll persuade Prunella not to live in Lenton, but murder—"

"I don't mean actual murder, silly. I mean a story about a murder – or two murders – in the old barn. A sort of local legend."

"I get it!" whooped Titch. "We tell Prunella this true story we made up and she won't fancy moving into the old barn, right?"

Shaz nodded. "Something like that."

"And who's going to do it?" asked Mickey.

"You?"

"Sure. It was my idea, so I do the job."

Titch looked at him. "When?"

"Well, it'll have to be next Tuesday, won't it? When Prunella comes to the library."

"Yeah," growled Mickey. "If she comes. They had a row, remember?"

"She might come before Tuesday," suggested Jillo. "You know – to make it up."

"Possibly," nodded Mickey. "We'll just have to keep our eyes skinned – watch the road for her car."

"Fine," said Jillo. "And now, if you two – sorry Raider, you three – have nothing else to do, Titch and I have something to show you."

"What?" asked Shaz.

"Oh, nothing much," said Jillo. "Only that brand new gang hut Mum and Dad promised us."

CHAPTER 5

SOME HQ!

"Hut?" gasped Shaz, gazing at the structure which stood in a corner of the Denton's paddock. "It's more like a palace."

"Well, not quite," smiled Jillo modestly. "But it's not bad, is it?"

"It's brilliant," said Mickey. "Absolutely brilliant." The hut's pine planking glistened, fragrant with fresh creosote. There were two large windows, one each side of the door, which was fitted with a stout mortise lock. The roof, clad in thick green felt, sloped down towards the back of the structure. A stub of iron stovepipe protruded at one end. Shaz pointed to this. "Hey, look, Mickey – it's even got heating!"

Jillo produced a shiny key and opened the door. Inside was a large wooden table and six

chairs. On the table stood two oil lamps. The floorboards were pale and smooth and at one end, on a plinth of brick, stood a fat black stove. On top of the stove a saucepan gleamed, and a brand new kettle.

"Well?" grinned Titch. "What d'you think?"

"What do I think?" breathed Mickey. "I think it's magic, Titch. Unbelievable. You've got terrific parents, kid."

"Yeah." Shaz nodded. "Fancy them doing all this, just for us."

"They promised, didn't they?" said Jillo. "When we saved the Roman hoard. They said we'd get a headquarters when everything was settled, and here it is."

Mickey shook his head. "This is some HQ, Jillo! If old Kilchaffinch had this, he wouldn't need to convert his crummy old barn."

"I vote we get some paint and put the oath on the wall," said Titch.

"Yeah," cried Shaz. "And we could paint a notice on the door: HQ THE OUTFIT – no admittance."

"Especially to miserable old farmers," added Titch, "and loopy librarians and their snobby girlfriends."

"I wonder who you mean?" growled Jillo.

Mickey grinned. "I was wondering what we could do till next Tuesday," he said. "Now I know – we'll spend the time fixing this place up."

"We'll need logs," said Titch. "Wood for the stove so we can do tea and soup and stuff."

"Curtains over the windows," suggested Shaz. "So snoopers can't look in."

"Rugs," said Mickey. "To keep our feet warm in winter."

"Pictures on the wall," put in Jillo.

"Not pictures – maps," contradicted Titch.

"HQs always have maps."

"A basket for Raider," said Mickey. "By the stove." Raider, busy sniffing every corner of the hut, yapped his approval.

"It seems we're going to be pretty busy," said Jillo. "I hope we don't get so wrapped up in this place we forget we're supposed to be saving Froglet Pond."

"No chance," snorted Mickey, and Shaz shook his head.

"I'm dreaming up a really horrific old legend about that barn," he said. "I can't wait to share it with Prunella."

Jillo smiled and nodded. "Good. Now, before we go any further, I'd better give everybody their key." She took three identical keys from her jacket pocket and handed them out. "Guard them with your lives," she hissed.

They walked all round the outside of the hut, admiring it from various angles till they'd had their fill, then set off to borrow saws and hatchets from the farm so they could start a woodpile.

CHAPTER 6

BITS OF WOMAN

Fixing the hut made the days fly, and before anybody had time to get bored it was Tuesday again. Kenneth and Prunella had not met in the meantime to patch up their quarrel but they had spoken on the phone, and to Shaz's relief Prunella showed up as usual that Tuesday at a quarter to twelve.

Shaz, the only child in the library, was sitting at one of the study tables pretending to scribble notes in a jotter. The table was strewn with books on local history he'd pulled from the shelves. The librarian, who had been glaring at him resentfully ever since he'd arrived, turned with a soppy smile to greet his love. Shaz pulled a face and looked down as the couple kissed.

Prunella glanced around. "Quiet, as usual," she remarked.

"Yes, my love," simpered Kenneth. "If it were not for our industrious little friend over there, we'd have the place to ourselves."

Prunella looked across at Shaz. "What's he doing?"

Kenneth shook his head. "I haven't a clue. He's wrecking – I mean, he's using the local history section, so it's probably a school project."

"But it's the holidays, dearest."

"Is it? Oh, well – I dunno, then. Ask him if you're interested."

Kenneth straightened a pile of leaflets on the counter as Prunella crossed the library. "Hello."

Shaz looked up into her smile. "Hi."

"What's your name?"

"Shaz. Shazad Butt, Miss."

"You look very busy, Shaz. What're you doing?"

"Project," Shaz grunted. "Holiday project. For school."

"Ah." Prunella tilted her head, trying to read the jotter. "What's it about?"

"Local legends."

"How interesting. Has Lenton got lots of

legends, Shaz?"

"A few."

"And they're all in these books, eh?"

Shaz shook his head. "Not all. I can't find anything about the barn murders."

"Barn murders?" Prunella pulled a face. "Sounds gruesome, Shaz. What exactly were the barn murders?"

Shaz shrugged. "A farmer's supposed to have gone mad a hundred years ago and killed his wife and daughter in a barn. Chopped 'em in bits with an axe. The barn's still there – we call it the haunted barn – but there's nothing in the books about it."

"Ugh!" Prunella shuddered. "Where is this barn, Shaz? I shall have to make sure I stay well away from it." She smiled. "Have you been inside?"

"Oooh, no, Miss." Shaz shivered. "It's on Kilchaffinch Farm but nobody goes inside. Nobody."

Prunella stiffened. "Kilchaffinch Farm?"

"Aye, Miss. It's that ruin by Froglet Pond." He grimaced. "They say if you go there at midnight there's blood running down the walls and bits of woman all over the — here, are you all right, Miss?"

Miss didn't look all right. White-faced and quivering, she sank into a chair "Water," she murmured. "A glass of water, please." The librarian was staring across at them.

Shaz rose and called out, "Mr Kilchaffinch, I think the lady's ill. Maybe we should…"

Kenneth was round the counter at once, striding towards them with a cry of "Sweetheart!"

"Don't call me sweetheart," muttered Shaz, cramming the jotter in his pocket. "Shall I—?"

"Go!" hissed the librarian. "Just go and leave us alone." He bent over Prunella.

"Yes, Mr Kilchaffinch," murmured Shaz. He left on tiptoe, managing not to laugh till he got outside.

CHAPTER 7

APE-SHAPE

They were all in the hut by two o'clock, seated round the table. Raider sat next to Mickey. Titch laughed. "You can spot the dog," she railed. "He's the intelligent one."

"Belt up, Titch," said Mickey. "This is Shaz's day."

"How'd it go?" asked Jillo.

"Swingingly," grinned Mickey. "Tell 'em, Shaz."

Shaz told them what had happened at the library. "She swallowed it," he chuckled. "The whole story. You should've seen her face when she realized I was talking about her new home. I nearly blew the whole thing laughing."

"I was lurking outside according to plan," put in Mickey. "I saw Shaz go off, and then I had quite a wait till Prunella and Kenneth came out. In fact, I'd begun to think they weren't coming. When they did, she was leaning on his arm looking fragile and he was yammering away at her, trying to convince her there's no such legend and the barn's not haunted at all. She didn't believe him though, because she'd said, 'You'll say anything, Kenneth Kilchaffinch, to persuade me to live in Lenton.' Anyway, I tailed 'em to Prunella's car, earwigging. I didn't catch every word but I did hear two important things." He paused, looking at the faces round the table.

"Well, go on," snapped Titch. "Share it."

"Number one," said Mickey, "Kenneth's desperate to prove the old barn's not haunted, so he's bullied Prunella into going there with him just before midnight tonight. And number two, Prunella's taken a room at the Fox and Pheasant. She wants to be handy to supervise the wedding preparations."

"Oh, wow!" groaned Jillo. "That's not good for us, is it? I mean, if she's staying at the pub she's more or less decided to stay in Lenton, right?"

Mickey shook his head. "Not necessarily, Jillo. And anyway, we haven't finished with her yet."

"What we gonna do?" queried Titch.

"Well, the first thing we're going to do is be at the old barn at midnight. We're gonna prove it's haunted."

"Midnight?" Titch shook her head. "We can't get out at midnight, Mickey. Dad'd go ape-shape."

Mickey shrugged. "If you two can't make it, Shaz and me'll go. It's too good an opportunity to miss, Titch."

"We'll try," promised Jillo. "We'll sneak out if we possibly can. I don't want to miss the fun."

Shaz chuckled. "It will be fun, too – scaring the pants off that grotty couple."

Mickey nodded. "It'll be fun if it works, but it'll only work if we've got a plan. Listen..."

CHAPTER 8

MIDNIGHT

It is ten minutes before midnight. A wind has arisen, driving drizzle in volleys against the glistening walls of the old barn, blowing rags of cloud from west to east so that a pale slice of moon seems to hurry in the opposite direction. Beyond the barn looms Weeping Wood. It sighs, breathing in and out like a squat, black monster as the wind shakes its treetops.

Inside the barn, four small figures huddle round the light from a pencil-torch. Two of these figures wear white nighties over day clothes. Another has his trouser legs stuffed down wellies and wears a battered hat. The fourth figure is dressed normally and carries a candle in one hand and a box of matches in the other. The four whisper together then separate, moving off to various parts of the great dark barn.

At one minute to midnight, Kenneth Kilchaffinch stopped the Land Rover's engine, switched off the lights and jumped down clutching a large black umbrella. He opened the umbrella and went round to the passenger side, his boots squelching in the mud by the field gate. "Come on," he said gruffly. "We're going to kill off this silly tale once and for all."

Prunella opened her door and stepped down, wishing she was safe in her bed. "Ugh!" she protested. "It's all sloppy. My shoes will be ruined."

"Not my fault," growled her lover. "I told you to wear wellies."

"I haven't got any wellies," snapped Prunella. "We don't wear wellies in town."

"Town!" spat Kenneth. "You're forever going on about town, Prunella. We don't do this in town, we don't do that in town. What the heck *do* you do in town? That's what I'd like to know."

"Well, we don't wade across horrible muddy fields at midnight in the rain," whined Prunella, "looking for the ghosts of murdered farmers' wives."

"Murdered granny!" cried Kenneth. "I told you, there are no ghosts. That kid was giving you a load of phoney baloney." He grabbed her wrist, pulled her under the umbrella and set off up the field.

They were about fifty metres from the barn when Prunella stopped dead. "Look!" She wouldn't budge, so Kenneth had to stop, too.

"What?"

"A light. I saw a light in the barn."

"Did you, heck! I can't see anything."

"I tell you I saw it. See – there it is again."

"Hmmm." This time Kenneth had seen it, too – a brief but unmistakable glimmer through a window. As the couple watched, another window shone briefly, then faded.

"S-someone's moving about in there," creaked Prunella. "One of the ghosts."

"A tramp, more likely," snarled Kenneth, "looking for a place to sleep. Come on."

"What're you going to do?"

"Kick him out, of course."

"Why – what harm's he doing?"

"He could start a fire – burn the place down."

"Good!" cried Prunella. "I wish he would, then perhaps we could live in town like civilized— look! Look there!" Kenneth shot her an exasperated glance. "Now what's the matter?"

Kenneth looked and saw two figures in white moving slowly across the barn's doorless entrance. He peered at them, frowning, then scoffed.

"It's those kids," he grated. "They must've heard me say we were coming here tonight. Well, I'll show them!"

He started forward. Prunella grabbed his sleeve. "Be careful, Kenneth – they don't look like kids to me."

"Gerroff!" He shook himself free and began running towards the barn.

Shaz, watching through a window, saw him coming. "Look out!" he yelled. "He's not fooled – he's after us." He blew out his candle, dropped it and made a dash for the door. The girls were already out, pelting towards the woods with their nighties flapping. Shaz followed and close behind came Mickey, clomping in his wellies, holding his hat on with his hand.

"Come here, you horrible brats!" cried

Kenneth. He was gaining on them. "I'll tear your heads off. I'll kick you from here to the village pond. I'll flatten the lot of you, see if I don't."

They beat him to the fence but it was a desperately close thing. Titch was last over, and as she rolled off the top rail Kenneth lunged, grabbing a handful of her nightie which tore as she fled into the trees, leaving the panting librarian slumped across the fence with a rag of white cotton in his fist.

CHAPTER 9

FAN-FLIPPIN'-TASTIC!

Wednesday morning, ten o'clock. Mickey, Shaz and Raider were already at the hut when Jillo and Titch appeared. Shaz grinned at them. "You two look absolutely shattered, but you obviously got back in all right."

Jillo nodded. "No problem. Mum and Dad sleep like logs once they drop off, but we are tired – we couldn't get to sleep for shaking."

"Right," nodded Mickey. "I was the same. I kept seeing Kenneth getting bigger and bigger behind us. Let's face it, folks – it was a disaster. An absolute disaster."

"It was fan-flippin'-tastic!" laughed Shaz. "Old Kenneth, pelting up the field waving his arms – he must've been furious he didn't catch us. He knows it was us but he can't prove it."

Jillo nodded. "You're right, Shaz – it was

fantastic. Titch came up with a brilliant excuse for her torn nightie – told Mum she had this nightmare where she had to fight a monster. Our trick might not have worked, but the whole thing was pretty funny when you look back." She grinned. "I know – why don't we go down the library, see what mood he's in? Wind him up a bit?"

"We know what mood he's in," chuckled Mickey. "Foul as always, only more so. It'll be a laugh, though – especially when he sees old Shaz."

They trooped into the library at twenty past ten. The children's section was deserted. Kenneth was sitting on a stool with his elbows on the counter and his head in his hands. He looked up as they entered. "Hoi!" He pointed at Raider. "You can't bring that in here."

"Why not?" asked Mickey. "He's on a lead, and anyway he's come to join."

"Don't be ridiculous."

"I'm not. He's an ace reader. In fact he's called Reader. People think it's Raider but it's Reader, really."

Kenneth rose to his feet. One corner of his

mouth was twitching. "Don't be impertinent. And you!" He glared at Shaz. "You're barred."

"How d'you mean, barred?" Shaz looked dismayed.

"Barred," snarled the librarian. "B-A-R-R-E-D. You are no longer welcome in this library."

"You can't do that!" cried Titch. "He's a member."

"Oh yes I can," smirked Kenneth. "I have the power to bar anyone who misbehaves on these premises."

"But I haven't misbehaved," protested Shaz. "I was doing research."

"You were telling lies to a lady. You told her a so-called legend about some murders in a barn. No such murders ever took place, and there is no such legend. And you were there last night – all of you – dressed up like Hallowe'en. You deliberately tried to frighten her."

Shaz shook his head. "We weren't out last night, Mr Kilchaffinch. It was a good night on the telly, wasn't it, folks?"

They nodded. "Superb," murmured Mickey.

"Don't you dare mock me," snarled the librarian, "or you'll be sorry."

Shaz grinned. "We wouldn't mock you,

41

Mr Kilchaffinch. You're too good a runner – especially on mud, uphill, at night."

Kenneth was round the corner like a flash, but Shaz was quicker. "Sorry," he cried. "Can't stop – I'm barred." He dodged the librarian's furious lunge. The Outfit turned and ran.

CHAPTER 10

MISERABLE SO-AND-SO

"There's something I don't get," said Titch, as she and Jillo made their way home for lunch.

"I know," chuckled Jillo. "Burger and chips for lunch every day. I don't get it, either."

"No, listen. It's nearly the end of July, right?" Jillo nodded.

"Kenneth and Prunella are supposed to get married the first week in September, aren't they?"

"Yes."

"And that's about six weeks from now, right?"

"Right. So?"

"So they'll be married in six weeks and old Reuben hasn't even started converting the barn yet. It takes longer than six weeks to convert a barn, surely?"

" 'Course it does, you div," scoffed Jillo. "It takes months."

"Well – where are they going to live till it's finished, Jillo?"

"Kilchaffinch Farm of course, with Reuben."

"How d'you know?"

"I heard Mum and Dad talking."

"Oh. So Froglet Pond might still be okay in September?"

"It might be." Jillo grinned. "D'you know why the wedding's in September?"

"No, why?"

"Two reasons. One: holiday flights are cheaper in September, so the honeymoon'll cost less, and two: all the kids'll be back at school. There'll be none outside the church so Kenneth won't have to throw pennies to them."

"Pennies?" Titch's eyebrows went up. "I didn't know they threw pennies at weddings."

"Oh, yes, bridegrooms do. Mum says they used to do it everywhere, but now it's just in Lenton."

"And Kenneth's getting married in September so he won't have to?"

"So Dad reckons."

"The miserable so-and-so. I hope the vicar

gets in a muddle and marries him to old Reuben by mistake."

Jillo laughed. "I think we should wag off – the whole school – and be there. It'd ruin his whole day."

"Hey!" Titch's eyes sparkled. "I've just had an idea."

"What?"

"Well – throwing pennies is a wedding custom, right?"

"Right."

"And if there's one custom, why shouldn't there be two?"

"What are you on about, Titch?"

"Listen." The two girls stopped while Titch whispered in her sister's ear. When they set off again, Jillo could hardly walk straight for laughing.

CHAPTER 11

AT THE DuCKING

"That's brilliant!" cried Mickey, as Jillo finished speaking. "How d'you think 'em up, that's what I'd like to know?"

"I didn't," admitted Jillo. "It was Titch, but she did the slug one so it's my turn."

Shaz nodded. "Prunella won't recognize you. When are you thinking of doing it?"

Jillo smiled. "What's wrong with this evening? Prunella gets back from the city around half six. I'll hang about near the pub and nobble her when she gets out of the car."

"What'll you say?" asked Titch.

Jillo shrugged. "Dunno. I'll think of something. You lot can tidy this place up and get the kettle on. I should be back around seven."

It was twenty-five to seven when Prunella's white Micra swept into the car park of the Fox and Pheasant. It was a warm, bright evening at the end of a sweltering afternoon, and for once Prunella was glad to be out of the city. She'd shopped after work, and three parcels sat beside her on the passenger seat. As she got out and began unloading the packages a child appeared, smiling.

"Hello. I'm Jill, but everybody calls me Jillo. Would you like a hand with the parcels?"

Prunella beamed. "That's extremely kind of you, Jillo. I thought I was going to have to make two trips. D'you think you can manage this one?"

"No problem, Miss." Jillo took the parcel. It was large and soft and crackly. Jillo smiled. "Is this your wedding dress, Miss?"

"What?" Prunella, her arms full of packages, was closing the car door with her bottom. "Oh, no, dear. No. It is a dress, but not a wedding dress." She looked sidelong at Jillo as they crossed the car park. "How did you know I was getting married?"

Jillo grinned. "Oh, everybody knows, Miss. That's what it's like in Lenton – everybody

knows everything. You're marrying Mr Kilchaffinch, aren't you?"

"That's right. Do you know him, Jillo?"

"Oh, yes, Miss. All the kids know Mr Kilchaffinch." She felt like adding "Because he's the most miserable pig in Lenton," but she didn't. Instead she smiled wistfully. "I wish I was coming to your wedding, Miss. I love weddings."

"Yes, well I'm afraid that won't be possible, dear. It's on a Wednesday in September at eleven o'clock in the morning. You'll be at school."

"I know, worst luck." They'd reached the

big swing doors. Prunella butted one and stood propping it open while Jillo passed into the red-carpeted hallway. There was a counter and some chairs.

"Just put the parcel on a chair, dear," said Prunella, dumping her own. "I can manage from here."

Jillo set down the package and treated Prunella to her sunniest smile. "I really don't mind missing the wedding, Miss, 'cause I'll see you in your dress at the ducking."

Prunella blinked. "Ducking?"

"Yes, Miss. You know – on Hallowe'en."

Prunella shook her head. "I'm afraid I haven't the faintest idea what you're taking about, dear. Ducking? Hallowe'en? What d'you mean?"

"Oh, Miss – you mean he hasn't told you?" Jillo giggled. "P'raps I'd best keep my mouth shut."

"No." Prunella shook her head. "No, I think you'd better go on. What about Hallowe'en, Jillo?"

"Well, you see, Miss, on Hallowe'en, the year's brides – them that's wed since last Hallowe'en – has to get in their bridal gowns and be taken down the village pond."

"Who takes them?" enquired Prunella, sharply.

"Why, Miss, their husbands of course, and all the village men. They takes 'em down the pond and chucks 'em in one by one to see if they float."

"Float?" croaked Prunella.

"Yes, Miss." Jillo smiled. "You see once, a long long time ago, a witch came to Lenton. Nobody knowed she's a witch and she married a local lad. After, she done all sorts of wicked mischief, making the cattle fall sick and horses to stumble and pigs to fly and all like that. They caught her in the end, mind – drownded her in the pond – but ever since then they ducks the brides at Hallowe'en to test if they be witches, 'cause a witch'll float and a true bride sinks. 'Course," Jillo winked, "no one believes in witches any more, but they keeps up the custom 'cause it's a bit of fun, like."

"A bit of fun. Yes." Prunella didn't smile. She was biting her lower lip. Her voice sounded funny, as though she was saying one thing and thinking another. "Well – thank you for telling me, Jillo. Thank you very much. And thanks for your help with the parcels, too.

Goodbye, dear."

" 'Bye, Miss." Jillo slipped away. She didn't like the look on Prunella's face, and she wouldn't have stood in Kenneth Kilchaffinch's shoes tonight for all the tea in China.

CHAPTER 12

DEAREST

When Jillo had gone, Prunella carried her purchases up to her room, unwrapped them and put them away. Then she washed, changed and did her hair. She didn't hum, sing or whistle while she was doing these things. She worked silently, keeping her lips compressed. It took her three-quarters of an hour. When she'd finished she went down to the hallway, put her key on the counter and left the Fox and Pheasant.

Kenneth Kilchaffinch was near the kitchen window when the white Micra pulled into the farmyard. He'd had a trying day at the library. Noticing a sticky red smear on a book, he'd opened it to find that somebody had been using a jam sandwich as a bookmark. As if this outrage wasn't enough, the guilty party had actually come back later and asked for his sandwich, and had thrown a tantrum when told it was in the bin. A trying day, but now Kenneth smiled, as he always did on first catching sight of his beloved. He went and stood in the doorway to watch her cross the yard, smiling at the way she trod a dainty path between mud slicks and hen-droppings.

"Hello, dearest," he smarmed as she drew near.

"Good evening, Kenneth."

The starchiness of her response sounded a warning bell in the librarian's brain. He broadened his smile as Prunella swept past him into the kitchen.

"Is something the matter, my love?"

"Where's your father?" Kenneth had tried hard to get her to call old Reuben Dad, but she wouldn't.

"He's drowning kittens in the toolshed."

"Ugh!"

"Everybody's entitled to a hobby, sweetest. Were you wanting him?"

"Hardly," said Prunella, tartly. "I hoped we'd be alone, and we are. Tell me about Hallowe'en."

"Ha – Hallowe'en, my love? Whatever do you—?"

"TELL ME ABOUT HALLOWE'EN!"

"I – I – well, Hallowe'en occurs on the thirty-first of October. It's also known as—"

"I KNOW WHAT HALLOWE'EN IS, KENNETH. TELL ME WHAT HAPPENS IN LENTON ON HALLOWE'EN!"

"Well, dearest, the children – not all the children, but some of them – dress as ghosts and things carry pumpkin lanterns and go round—"

"THE POND, KENNETH. TELL ME ABOUT THE POND!"

"Pond." Kenneth was becoming confused. "Oh – the pond. Yes. Well, you're not to worry about the pond, my sweet. Dad's going to have it drained and filled in well before—"

"NOT THAT POND, KENNETH. THE VILLAGE POND."

"The village pond, my angel? Whatever can my darling wish to know about the village pond?"

Prunella gazed at him for several seconds in silence, then she took a deep breath and spoke, very quietly and very slowly. "I will say to you the word BRIDES, Kenneth. I want you to put the word BRIDES together with the words POND and HALLOWE'EN, and tell me if they suggest something to you – something you've forgotten to mention to me, perhaps. Something I ought to know." She lowered herself into a chair, gazing at her bewildered fiancé. He stared back, his mind in a whirl, his mouth agape. He didn't know what to say. He had no idea what Prunella expected him to say. He wondered if she had gone mad. After a long, long minute she said, "You look exactly like a cod, Kenneth. A dead cod. Have you nothing at all to say to me?"

"I – don't understand, my precious. I was looking forward to our evening together. I was going to suggest the Pizza Hut, and then a film. There's a good one on at the Odeon, I believe."

"I see," purred Prunella. "And I suppose afterwards, if we want even more fun, you could fling me into the village pond to see if I float. It's not too far from the Odeon, is it?"

"Prunella?" Perhaps she was ill. He started towards her.

"STAY AWAY FROM ME!"

"But, dearest," he protested. "I'm worried.

Can't you see how worried I am?"

"Not worried enough to tell me the truth, evidently. Well," Prunella rose, "you needn't worry any more on my account, Kenneth Kilchaffinch, because I'm leaving. I'm leaving this house, I'm leaving Lenton and I'm leaving YOU." She marched to the door. He reached for her but she knocked his arm away. Stricken, he could only watch as she crossed the yard, got into the car and roared away, leaving him to moan the word "dearest" at a cloud of blue exhaust.

CHAPTER 13

FETCH 'ER BACK

"What am I going to do, Dad?" Reuben Kilchaffinch eased his foot out of a muddy boot and hurled it into a corner. "You shoulda done what I done with your mother, lad, right from the start."

"What's that, Dad?"

"Keep 'er in line, that's what. Women!" He hurled the other boot. "Give 'em an inch and they'll walk all over you."

"But she's gone, Dad. Left me. I can't keep her in line if she's not here, can I?"

"Well, don't stand there whining then. Get after her. Fetch 'er back. And when you get 'er up here, give 'er some stick."

"Is that how you handled Mum?"

"Aye."

"And it worked?"

" 'Course it worked."

"But she's not here now, Dad."

"No. She waited till my back were turned and ran off with a crackpot scientist. Didn't know where she was well off."

Kenneth groaned. "So it didn't work, Dad, did it?" He shook his head. "She was talking crazy talk, Dad. Hallowe'en. Brides. The pond. You should've heard her."

Reuben spread dripping on a hunk of bread, crammed it in his mouth and talked through it, spraying greasy crumbs down the front of his jersey. "Sounds to me like somebody's been talking to 'er again, lad – having 'er on. It'll be that kid, or one of his mates."

"But why, Dad? Why would kids go out of their way to upset a lovely young woman like Prunella? What could they possibly get out of it?"

The old man shrugged. "Who knows with kids? I reckon they're at the bottom of all this bother, though. Stands to reason." He dunked bread and dripping in his tea and waved it about. "If I was you I'd get onto 'em, find out what their little game is and give 'em the biggest walloping of their lives. That'll learn 'em."

"I will!" Kenneth slammed his right fist into his left palm. "By golly I will. I'll flush 'em out, force a confession out of them that'll get Prunella back, and when I've finished with them they'll really wish they'd never been born."

Reuben cackled, dribbling wet bread. "That's the way, lad. Kittens and kids. They all want drownin'."

CHAPTER 14

NEWTS

The following morning a boy called Jason Mason crept nervously into the library. He hated being there, but he had a holiday assignment to write and he needed to borrow some books. He lingered in the doorway, combing his hair with his fingers and checking his trainers for mud. He knew that the librarian would yell at him, chase him on to the street and bar him if he saw anything which displeased him. Jason was straightening the tie he'd put on especially when Kenneth Kilchaffinch noticed him.

"Come on in, lad," he beamed. "Nobody's going to eat you."

Jason grinned sheepishly and approached the counter, wondering if he was walking into a trap. The librarian rubbed his big red hands together, smiling benignly over his glasses.

"Now – what can we do for you, young man? A good, exciting story, eh? Or are we looking for something a little more serious?"

"Er – serious, please," murmured Jason. "I have to do an assignment on newts."

"Newts!" Kenneth spoke the word so enthusiastically you'd have thought half his family were newts. "Well now, let me see … ah, yes. Over here, I think." He led the boy to a rack of immaculately-shelved non-fiction. Running a finger along the neat row of spines, he began pulling volumes out and piling them on a table. Soon there were nine books on the pile.

Jason giggled nervously. "I – I'm only allowed three, Mr Kilchaffinch. It says so on my card." He still couldn't believe the librarian wasn't going to turn suddenly and smack him in the mouth.

"Nonsense!" cried Kenneth, jovially. "Rules are made to be broken, lad, didn't you know that?"

"No – no, Mr Kilchaffinch, I didn't."

"Oh, yes. The rule says three books, I say nine. You'll find everything you need to know about newts in these."

Jason nodded. "Th – thanks, Mr Kilchaffinch. Thanks a lot." He giggled again. "I don't know how I'm going to get all these read in two weeks."

"Two weeks?" Kenneth's eyebrows went up. "Why should you have to read them in two weeks?"

"Well – you can only borrow for two weeks. It says so on—"

"Whoa!" Kenneth laughed. "What did I just say about rules, lad?"

"Oh, yes. I forgot."

"You forgot! Keep 'em for three weeks. Four. Keep 'em for five if you like, only try not to use jam sandwiches for bookmarks, there's a good lad." He grinned. "Shall I tell you something – something you won't find in any of those books?"

"Yes please, Mr Kilchaffinch."

"Right, well listen. It's about newts. There are three species of newts in Britain. You'll find their names in the books. One of them – the great crested newt – is becoming quite rare, but I know a place not a million miles from here where you can still find some."

"You do? Where's that, Mr Kilchaffinch?"

"Ever heard of Froglet Pond?"

" 'Course. Everybody has."

"Well – that's where they are."

"Really? I've been there loads of times and I've never seen 'em."

Kenneth shook his head. "You won't. They keep themselves well hidden, but you can find 'em once you know they're there."

"Wow – thanks, Mr Kilchaffinch! I'll go look – maybe take some photos for my assignment." He grinned. "I bet I get an A for it."

Kenneth smiled and nodded. "I'm glad I could help – er – what is your name, lad?"

"Jason, Mr Kilchaffinch. Jason Mason."

"I'm glad I could help, Jason." He smiled. "Actually, there's something you could help me with, if you would."

" 'Course, Mr Kilchaffinch. What is it?"

Kenneth smiled. "A bit of information, lad, that's all. Just a bit of information about some school mates of yours."

CHAPTER 15

JUST FOR FUN

Kenneth presided over his almost-deserted library till lunchtime, then put an assistant in charge and gave himself the afternoon off. With Jason Mason's sketch map to guide him, he had no difficulty in locating the Denton's paddock and the hut that occupied a corner of it. He seemed to be in luck, too, because the door stood ajar. He was about to catch the so-called Outfit unawares.

Smiling unpleasantly, the librarian sidled up to the door and flung it open. Raider, who had been lying in wait, seized his trouser-leg and tugged, pulling Kenneth off balance so that he crashed to the floor like a felled giraffe as The Outfit yelled "Surprise!"

Five seconds passed while Kenneth lay stunned on the threadbare rug by the door.

Then he groaned, lifted his head and shook it. Four solemn faces looked down at him. He closed his eyes and let his head fall back.

"You'll pay for this," he gasped. "You've messed around with Kenneth Kilchaffinch once too often." He rolled on his side, retrieved his glasses and clambered to his feet. The Outfit stood bunched watching him. He brushed his jacket with his hand and gazed at them. "I take it you were expecting me?"

Mickey nodded. "Tip-off from a mate of ours, Mr Kilchaffinch. Jason, they call him. He's doing an assignment on newts."

"Yes, well. You were in enough trouble as it was, without setting your dog on me."

"We didn't set him on you," protested Titch. "He's still mad because he didn't get to join the library."

Kenneth snorted. "You know, your parents are going to be pretty mad, too, when I tell them what you've been up to."

"What have we been up to?" asked Shaz, innocently.

"Creeping about at midnight, playing with matches, trespassing on other people's property."

"Who, us?" cried Jillo. "Where? When, for goodness' sake?"

"You know where and when. And then there are the lies you've told my fiancée, frightening her with silly tales about slugs and ghosts and Hallowe'en." He gave Mickey a baleful stare. "What was that about Hallowe'en and brides and the pond, anyway."

"Hallowe'en?" Mickey shrugged. "Brides? Pond? I'm afraid I don't know what you mean, Mr Kilchaffinch."

"Not much you don't! I've no idea why you've done these things, but I'll tell you what happens next. You're going to write a letter to my fiancée, admitting that your stories were totally untrue and apologizing for the distress they've caused her."

"You're joking," said Mickey.

"I never joke."

"We won't do it."

"You'll also admit it was you she saw at the barn the other night. You'll all sign the letter, and you'll stay away from my fiancée and myself from now on. If you refuse, I'll go to your—"

He broke off, staring at a poster on the wall. "What does that mean – Froglet Pond for ever?"

"Froglet Pond's part of Lenton's heritage," said Jillo. "Nobody has the right to destroy it."

"The pond's on my father's land!" blustered Kenneth. "He has the right."

Jillo shook her head. "He has the power," she said. "It's not the same. The Outfit aims to save Froglet Pond for the people of Lenton, and for the creatures which live in it."

"Ah!" Kenneth gazed at the poster and nodded. "Yes. Now I see. So that's your little game, is it?" He looked at them. "You thought that if you drove my fiancée away, the old barn wouldn't be converted and the pond needn't be drained. I'm right, aren't I?" He laughed harshly. "Of course I'm right. Well, you've failed, because if the lady has gone – and I wouldn't be in your shoes if she has – we'll just drain the pond anyway. We'll drain it JUST FOR FUN!"

CHAPTER 16

WRITE A LETTER – MAKE IT BETTER

What might have happened next, neither the children nor Kenneth Kilchaffinch would ever know, because at that moment a shadow fell across the doorway and Mr Denton looked in. "Oh, hello, Kenneth. Everything all right here, is it?"

The librarian shook his head. "No, I'm afraid it's not, Mr Denton. Could I have a word with you, please – in private?"

The farmer looked surprised, but nodded. "Yes, of course." He looked at the children. "Why not take Raider for a walk in the woods – scare a few rabbits?" He looked at his watch. "Give us half and hour."

"Oh, heck!" sighed Jillo, as the four stumped

69

into Weeping Wood. "Now it's all come out – Kenneth's version, that is. We're in dead trouble, folks."

Shaz smiled wanly. "Well – we're the guys who can handle it, Jillo. We're The Outfit, right?"

Jillo looked dubious. "You haven't seen Dad when he's upset, Shaz. It's not a pretty sight."

Only Raider enjoyed the woods and it was a subdued group that approached the hut when the farmer's half hour was up. The door stood open. Mr Denton was sitting at the table, looking grave. Kenneth Kilchaffinch had gone.

"Sit down, please," said the farmer quietly. They sat.

"Now." Mr Denton clasped his hands on the table and gazed at them, then peered at the children from beneath his shaggy eyebrows. "Mr Kilchaffinch has told me some disturbing stories about you people. He says you have been bombarding his fiancée with false information designed to discourage her from coming to live in Lenton. Is this true?"

"Bombarding's a bit strong," murmured Mickey. "We made up a few old legends and quaint local customs."

"You told her we cook with slugs, am I right?"

"Yes."

"You also said there were murders in the old barn on Kilchaffinch's land, didn't you?"

"Yes."

"And that it's haunted by the ghosts of the victims?"

"Right."

The farmer looked at Jillo. "Where were you at midnight on Tuesday, young woman?"

Jillo bit her lip and looked down. "At the old barn, Dad."

"And you took your little sister with you?"

"Yes."

"We were all there," put in Shaz. "Except Raider."

"And when Mr Kilchaffinch arrived to show his fiancée that your story about the place being haunted was nonsense, you proceeded to put on a show which was designed to frighten the pair of them away?"

Shaz giggled. "Yes, only it was us who ended up running."

Mr Denton frowned. "There's nothing even faintly amusing about any of this, young man. My daughters know full well that they are forbidden to leave the house after dusk, and I'm sure that if your parents – and your father, Michael – weren't away, they'd forbid you, too." The farmer's voice had risen as he spoke, till he was almost shouting. Now he sat back in his chair, shook his head and spoke quietly.

"I know why you people have acted the way you have, and I sympathize. Froglet Pond is important, and it is absolutely typical of Reuben Kilchaffinch to want to destroy it when there is no real reason to do so. However, the pond is on his land and he has the legal right to do whatever he wants with it. What I'm saying is, you are right in wanting to save it but wrong in the method you have chosen. We must not intimidate people, even in a just cause." The farmer paused and, for the first time, smiled. "If you look carefully, I'm sure you'll find another way of fighting for Froglet Pond, and in the meantime I think you ought to write a letter to the young woman and take it to Mr Kilchaffinch at the library."

He held up a hand as Mickey opened his mouth to protest. "I know you don't like the man – few people do – but Kenneth Kilchaffinch can't help being the way he is. He had a harrowing childhood which stunted his personality." He stood up.

"Write the letter – a letter of confession and apology – hand it to Mr Kilchaffinch and we'll say no more about the matter. Good afternoon to you."

"That was awful," murmured Shaz, when Mr Denton had gone.

Jillo shook her head. "We got off light, believe me."

"But we've lost, haven't we? Prunella gets our letter, agrees to live in Lenton after all and Froglet Pond's a goner."

Mickey shook his head. "Not necessarily, Shaz. Take it from me, we're not done yet. All is not lost. There are other weapons in our armoury. The Outfit fights on."

Shaz looked at him. "What other weapons? What're you on about, Mickey?"

"On about?" Mickey grinned. "I'm on about harrowing childhoods, lurking scientists and runaway mothers. I'm on about letters. But most of all, I'm on about newts."

"You're barmy," growled Shaz. "Come on, let's get it over with. Who's going to write this disastrous letter?"

CHAPTER 17

LONG LOST MOTHER – WRITE ANOTHER

They wrote it in rough with lots of crossings out and alterations. When they were satisfied with it, Jillo copied it out in her best handwriting while Titch went home for an envelope. There was a brief argument over who should take it to the library. In the end they all went except Raider, and were relieved to find an assistant at the counter. She told them Mr Kilchaffinch was on the phone and promised to give him the letter as soon as he was free.

"Well," sighed Shaz as they left the building. "Thank goodness that's over. Now what?"

"Back to headquarters," said Mickey. "I've got a story to tell you about our beloved librarian, and a plan of action."

His friends were curious and pressed him all the way back, but Mickey refused to enlighten them till they were all seated round the table in the hut.

"Right." He rubbed his hands together, smiling at their expectant faces. Even Raider had left his basket to join them. "You know what Mr Denton said about Kilchaffinch – that he had a harrowing childhood which stunted his personality?" The children nodded and Raider went "Yip".

"Well, I know what he was on about, because my dad told me."

"Well, come on," urged Titch. "Quit spinning it out and tell us."

"Okay. Once upon a time, when he was very small, Kenneth Kilchaffinch had a mother."

"No kidding!" scoffed Jillo. "I thought his dad found him under a gooseberry bush."

"No, listen. He had a mother, and she protected him from old Reuben because Reuben was a foul-tempered so-and-so even then, and he didn't like kids. So she protected little Kenneth but there was nobody to protect her, and Reuben led her a terrible life, as you can probably imagine. Anyway, one day a guy showed up at Kilchaffinch Farm – a sort of scientist. He was interested in Froglet Pond, and he managed to persuade Reuben to let him mess around for a week or two, studying it. Mrs Kilchaffinch started giving him tea and samples of her baking, and they fell in love."

"Oooh, yuk!" choked Jillo. "Excuse me while I'm sick."

"No, listen – this is what my dad told me, right? They fell in love, and when the guy left he took her with him, leaving the kid – he was only about four – to be brought up by Reuben."

"Oh, wow!" cried Shaz. "I'd rather be brought up by Dracula."

"I thought you *were*," grinned Titch. Shaz went to swipe her across the head but she ducked.

"So," continued Mickey, "Mummy ran off with her scientist and Daddy raised little Kenneth, which wasn't a bundle of laughs for little Kenneth. My dad reckons the kid spent half his time locked in the cellar with nothing to eat and once, when he was drunk, old Reuben put him on the bull and tried to make him ride, and he's been scared of cattle ever since. Anyway, that's why Kenneth's a bit peculiar, and that's what Mr Denton meant."

"This is all dead interesting, Mickey," said Jillo, "But what's it got to do with Froglet Pond?"

"I'm coming to that. Why d'you reckon the scientist was interested in the pond?"

"'Cause it's where the Loch Ness Monster goes for its holidays?" suggested Titch.

"Idiot! What's Jason Mason doing his assignment about?"

"Newts."

"And what did our stunted librarian tell him about Froglet Pond?"

"That there are great crested newts in it."

"Right. And that's why the scientist was interested. The great crested newt is an endangered species. It could die out. What d'you think might happen if that scientist found out that Reuben Kilchaffinch intends filling in Froglet Pond?"

"I dunno. What do you think?"

"I think he might try to stop him."

"Yes, but he won't find out, will he?"

"He will if we tell him."

"Do you know where he lives?"

"With Kenneth's mum."

"Do we know her address?"

"No, but we know a man who does." Mickey laughed. "I think we've got another letter to write."

CHAPTER 18

ENTERTAINMENT

"Dad? Where are you, Dad?"

At the sound of his son's voice, Reuben pulled the last leg off the fly he was torturing and dropped the creature on the windowsill. "I'm 'ere," he growled. "In the kitchen. What's up?"

"Nothing, Dad. You were right. Everything's going to be fine."

Reuben cackled. "Leather 'em did you, them brats?"

"Well, no – it wasn't necessary. I—"

"Necessary? What's necessary got to do with it, eh? Leatherin' kids is fun lad. Don't you believe in fun?"

"Well, yes, but – anyway, Dad, what I wanted to tell you was, I made 'em write a letter to Prunella admitting everything. She's not got it yet, of course, but I spoke to her on the phone and told her all about it and she's coming back."

"Good." Reuben snatched a fresh fly and plucked off its wings. "So you reckon we can start on the old barn, eh?"

Kenneth nodded. "I think so, yes." He chuckled nastily. "Let's do the pond first. Kids love that pond."

"Aye," nodded Reuben, amputating the fly's limbs one by one. "So did the fool wot ran off with your mother. I'll hire some pumping gear first thing Monday." He grinned. "It'll be nowt but a muddy hole by Tuesday night, lad. Wednesday I'll take the digger over and fill it in, and it'll be like there never was a Froglet Pond!" He chuckled. "Eeeh! – I'd love to see them frogs' faces when they show up next spring and their precious pond's gone. They'll be spawnin' all over the grass." This idea started the old farmer laughing and it was some time before he was able to control himself. When his mirth began to subside he pulled a grubby red handkerchief out of his pocket and mopped the tears from his cheeks. "Eeeh, lad," he gasped, "there's entertainment all round if you know where to look for it."

Kenneth nodded without smiling. He could remember his father laughing in just the same way when, as a toddler, he'd clung paralysed with terror to the coarse hair on the bull's back, jolting and swaying as the drunken Reuben walked the sullen beast round and round its pen. He turned and left the kitchen. The old man gazed after him for a moment, then scooped up his tally of legless flies and proceeded to flick them one after the other across the dingy kitchen.

CHAPTER 19

UP AND DOWN

"Hello, Dad? It's me – Mickey."

"Oh, hi, son. Is something wrong?"

"No, Dad. Me and Raider are fine. How's things with you?"

"Up and down, son. Up and down. What can I do for you?"

"I want to ask you something."

"Go ahead – I'm listening."

"Well, you know that story you told me a long time ago, about Mrs Kilchaffinch and the scientist?"

"Aye, I remember."

"And later on – years later – you told me you ran into them at Appleby or somewhere like that, in a pub?"

"That's right."

"And they told you where they were living?"

"Yes. What's all this about, Mickey?"

"Do you remember the address, Dad?"

"Aye. Why?"

"I need it. It's important."

"Is it now? What are you up to, son? Not chasing after baddies again in the middle of the night, I hope?"

"No, nothing like that. But it is important."

"Hmm. If I give it to you, do you promise you'll not use it to make mischief?"

"I promise."

"Okay, then. Have you got a pencil?"

"Yes."

"Write this down, then. The Old Brew House, Ten Yards Lane, Apton Magna, Bucks. Got that? And their name's Nichols."

"And they do still live there?"

"Far as I know, yes."

"Thanks, Dad. Thanks a lot. When d'you think you'll be coming home?"

"Can't tell, son. Depends how it goes. You know – business. Week or two yet, anyway. Might even be September."

"Okay, Dad. I'll see you when I see you."

" 'Bye, son. You take care now."

" 'Bye, Dad."

CHAPTER 20

REUBEN DOESN'T CARE

Dear Mr Nichols,

You don't know us. We call ourselves The Outfit and live in Lenton. We thought you might be interested in something that is happening here. Our librarian Mr Kilchaffinch is getting married and his dad, Reuben, is having the old barn converted into a house for Kenneth and his wife to live in. Near the barn is Froglet Pond, which has great crested newts in it. But Reuben doesn't care. He's going to drain the pond and fill it in. Kenneth says they're doing it for fun, but he wouldn't think it was fun if he was a great crested newt, would he? We want to save Froglet Pond, and we hope you can help.

P.S. We think Mr Kilchaffinch might make a better newt than he does a librarian, at that.

Yours sincerely
The Outfit

CHAPTER 21

SHE MUST BE MAD

Saturday morning, ten to nine. In Apton Magna, Professor Toby Nichols is going through his mail at the breakfast table. He holds up a blue envelope for his wife to see. "Child's handwriting, wouldn't you say?"

Ada Nichols, formerly Kilchaffinch, nods. "Looks like it, dear. Aren't you going to open it?"

"Postmark Lenton," muses the Professor. "Yes, of course I'm going to open it."

He slits the envelope, pulls out the letter, unfolds it and reads rapidly.

"Good grief!"

"What is it, dear?"

"Listen to this." He reads aloud. When he's finished, his wife pulls a face.

"I pity the poor girl, whoever she is. Marrying

Kenneth and moving in next door to Reuben. She must be mad."

The Professor nods. "I agree, but that's not the worst of it. Reuben means to drain the pond." He pushes back his chair, stands up and begins to pace. "It's vandalism, Ada. Sheer vandalism. He mustn't be allowed to get away with it."

"But what can we do, dear? It's on his land."

"Makes no difference. That pond's the only one for miles around that harbours the great crested newt. It ought to be a protected habitat, and I intend to see that it becomes one."

His wife nods grimly. "Good for you, Toby. Get on the phone. Talk to some people. And if you're thinking of going to Lenton yourself, I'll go with you. Froglet Pond's not the only thing around there that needs saving."

CHAPTER 22

SPEAK OF THE DEVIL

It was ten o'clock on Sunday morning when Mickey, Shaz and Raider arrived at the hut. The two girls were already there.

"Got the kettle on, then?" cried Mickey.

"No, we haven't," retorted Jillo. "You could put it on, only you'd have to light the stove first and the weather's a bit warm for that."

"Sure is, so let's forget it. We can't spare the time anyway."

"Why – where are we going?"

"Froglet Pond, of course. Gotta be ready to defend it in case old Reuben decides to start draining it before help arrives."

"D'you think help will arrive, Mickey?"

"'Course. Mr Nichols should've got our letter yesterday. He's not going to stand by and see the great crested newt wiped out, is he?"

Jillo shrugged. "Dunno, Buckinghamshire's a long way from Lenton."

"Well, we're here aren't we, so let's go and do what we can, right?"

They walked through Weeping Wood and stood gazing over the fence onto Kilchaffinch land. The pond lay bright and tranquil in the warm sunshine. Iridescent dragonflies darted back and forth across its surface, and now and then a swallow came swooping down to take a midge. Nobody was there.

"Not today, then," murmured Shaz.

Titch shook her head. "Sunday. Maybe old Reuben don't believe in working Sundays."

"You're joking," scoffed Jillo. "Old Reuben'd feed his granny into a sausage machine on a Sunday if somebody paid him to do it."

The boys had just cracked out laughing at this when Raider growled and yipped. "Oh-oh," groaned Mickey. "Speak of the devil."

A mud-spattered jeep had swung through the field gate and was bouncing towards them. Reuben was driving. Beside him sat a man they couldn't immediately identify. The vehicle stopped in front of the old barn. Both men got out. Mickey hissed Raider to silence and The Outfit crouched, watching.

"Who's the other feller?" whispered Jillo.

"I think it's Mr Partman," hissed Shaz. "You know – Partman the builder?"

Jillo nodded. "That figures. I suppose Mr Partman's going to do the work on the barn."

"Old Reuben must be in a hurry, too," murmured Mickey, "dragging him out here on a Sunday."

The two men walked slowly round the outside of the barn, stopping now and then while Mr Partman wrote in a notebook. When they'd been all the way round they went inside. "What're we going to do?" whispered Titch.

"I don't think there's anything we can do right now." Jillo told her. "Mr Partman's not going to start work today – he hasn't brought any equipment with him."

"No, and neither has old Reuben," said Shaz, "so the pond's probably safe for the moment, too, but we know it won't be long. We'd better be here really early tomorrow with some sort of plan."

"Yeah." Mickey gulped. "We're going to need a plan all right. A good one. Now that it's started it feels pretty scary, doesn't it?"

"Ah-ha," Jillo smiled wanly." We'll just have to be brave, Mickey, and hold the fort till Mr Nichols gets here."

"If he bothers to come," grunted Titch.

"He'll come," said Mickey, wishing he felt as sure as he sounded.

The two men emerged from the barn and climbed into the jeep, which coughed and roared away. The children watched till it disappeared through the gateway, then walked back through the wood. There wasn't much talk. Everybody was thinking about tomorrow when The Outfit would stand, alone if it must, in defence of Froglet Pond.

CHAPTER 23

WE DIDN'T MEAN TO, HONEST

It began at a quarter past ten on that Monday morning when Mickey, Jillo, Shaz and Titch, who had been keeping watch since eight o'clock, heard a tractor in the distance. In fact, Raider heard it first and alerted the others with a warning growl.

"Right." Mickey's firm tone disguised his nervousness. "Nobody's turned up to help, so we're on our own. Stick to the plan and we'll beat 'em easy. Let's go."

Their plan was simple. There was only one gateway to the field in which Froglet Pond and the old barn lay. In order to begin work on either, Reuben or Mr Partman or somebody would have to drive a vehicle through that gateway. As the sound of the tractor grew louder, The Outfit vaulted the fence and raced down the field. They arrived at the gateway seconds ahead of the tractor and threw themselves on the ground. It was extremely muddy, but the children had come in their oldest clothes.

Reuben picked his nose and whistled tunelessly through his snaggle teeth as he steered the tractor one-handedly into the gateway. The morning was bright and sunny, and he'd been looking forward to this all weekend. The tractor was towing a small trailer. On the trailer was the bright yellow diesel pump he'd hired in town. A few hours' work with the pump and Froglet Pond would cease to exist.

As the tractor swung into the gateway, Reuben let out a yell and hit the brake. The tractor stopped dead but the trailer skidded crabwise and tilted. The pump slid across the trailer, toppled, and landed with a thump in the mud. Reuben's eyes bulged out of his red face as he roared, "WHAT IN THE SCRUG-BUSTED RUMBLE POOP DO YOU LOT THINK YOU'RE PLAYING AT?"

Jillo raised her head. "We're The Outfit!" she cried, over the engine noise. "Froglet Pond

for ever!"

"FROGLET POND MY GRANNY!" screeched Reuben. "GET YER USELESS CARCASSES OUTA MY WAY OR I'LL SQUASH THE LOT O' YER!"

"No, you won't!" yelled Shaz. "Even you wouldn't dare run over a kid on purpose. You'd go to jail for ever."

"BY GAW!" Reuben switched off his engine and clambered down. "IF YER NOT GONNA MOVE I'LL SHIFT YER WITH MY 'OBNAILED BOOTS. I'LL KICK YER TO BITS AND STAMP ON THE PIECES. I'LL—"

"Up, Raider!" snapped Mickey. "Get 'im, boy!" Raider, who had been lying quietly beside Mickey, leapt to his feet and ran growling to meet the advancing farmer. Reuben aimed a kick at the dog, missed and retreated towards his vehicle. Only then did he see the pump in the mud.

"LOOK 'ERE!" he bellowed. "SEE WHAT YE'VE DONE. THAT'S 'IRED EQUIPMENT, THAT IS. YE'LL PAY FOR THIS, YOU SEE IF YOU DON'T." Stamping and fuming and with Raider snapping at his heels, he mounted the tractor, started it up, turned and drove off, leaving the pump where it had fallen.

"Hooray!" cried Titch, leaping to her feet. "We've won, we've won!"

Jillo sat up and shook her head. "Not yet we haven't, Titch. He'll be back, and this time he'll bring help."

"Maybe our help'll be here by then," said Shaz.

"Huh!" grunted Mickey.

It was more than half an hour before Reuben returned. The children spent the time pulling loose bits off the pump and hiding them. They watched out for Mr Nichols, too, but when they heard the tractor again he still hadn't come.

"Never mind," grated Jillo. "Down, everybody."

They lay down again, but this time it was no use. Kenneth had followed his father in the jeep, and when he got out he was carrying a shotgun.

"All right, you lot," he snarled. "On your feet. And you," he glared at Mickey, "keep that animal under control or I'll blow its head off, d'you hear?"

Mickey nodded, getting up. "He never really wanted to join your rotten library anyway."

They had to stand in a line with their hands on their heads while Kenneth helped Reuben lift the pump on to the trailer. When that was done, the librarian marched them across the field and made them line up against the barn wall while Reuben drove the tractor to the rim of Froglet Pond.

"Right." Kenneth smiled his nasty smile. "Now you can stand there and watch your precious pond disappear. And no tricks." He brandished the shotgun. "Remember, I've got this."

"He thinks he's in a film," whispered Shaz. They watched as father and son manoeuvred the trailer into position and ran out the pump's two lengths of hose – one into the pond and the other down the field. Then it was time to start the pump's diesel motor. Both men spent several minutes bending over the apparatus, which coughed and wheezed and belched out clouds of smoke but did not start. Mickey grinned and sneaked a look at his watch. "Come on, Mr Nichols," he muttered. "We can't hold out for ever."

No sooner were these words out than Kenneth straightened up and came stalking towards the children, cradling the gun and with a face like thunder. "All right," he grated. "What have you done with them?"

Mickey gazed at him, wide-eyed. "What?"

"You know what. The engine parts. Where are they?"

"Engine parts?" The boy shrugged. "We don't know anything about engine parts, Mr Kilchaffinch." He appealed to the others. "Do we, folks?" The three shook their heads.

Kenneth smiled thinly and looked at Raider, sitting at Mickey's feet. "Nice dog, that. What d'you call him – Raider, isn't it?"

Mickey shook his head. "Reader. He's a big Roald Dahl fan. In fact, he's halfway though *Charlie and the Chocolate Factory* at the moment."

Kenneth didn't smile. "Pity to lose a dog like that though, eh?"

"I won't lose him."

"Oh yes you will." The librarian lifted the gun and eased off the safety catch. "I'm going to count to three. If you haven't coughed up those engine parts by the time I get to three,

I'll shoot him where he sits." He raised the gun, tucking the stock into his shoulder and squinting along the barrel. "One."

Mickey bit his lip.

"Two."

Mickey's face was dead white. He swallowed and Titch blurted, "Tell him, Mickey!"

Kenneth chuckled. "You tell me, little girl."

Titch shook her head. "No."

"Three." The man's finger whitened on the trigger and a voice shrieked, "Kenneth – no!"

The librarian spun round as if he himself had been shot. Prunella was stumbling across the field, her coat flapping. "You can't," she cried. "You can't shoot a child, Kenneth."

"I wasn't – it was the dog, dearest. Only the dog."

"Only!" Prunella had reached him. She grabbed the weapon and jerked it from his grasp. "I thought I was marrying a librarian," she shrieked, "not some sort of gangster!" She threw the gun down as Kenneth reached out and circled her with his arms. "Get off!" she spat. "Don't you dare grab me, you ape!"

"Give 'er some stick!" croaked Reuben, jumping up and down beside the useless pump.

"I told you, lad – you can't beat the old stick for knockin' a bit o' sense into a wom—"

"You haven't changed one bit, have you, Reuben Kilchaffinch?"

The old farmer whirled round. Two figures had emerged from behind the barn. One was a man waving what looked like a sheaf of papers. The other was a woman waving what was unmistakably a sturdy umbrella. The woman reached Reuben first and began beating him about the head and shoulders. The farmer flung up his arms to shield himself, flinching and wincing as the umbrella rose and fell. "Lay off, Ada!" he yelped. "You're killing me, woman."

"I wish I were," grunted his ex-wife, swinging lustily as her umbrella began to disintegrate. "This is for all the stick you once gave me, you nasty-minded, smelly old goat."

Under the barn wall, The Outfit goggled in disbelief at this turn of events. "It's Kenneth's mum!" whooped Mickey. "And she's brought Mr Nichols!"

The man reached Reuben just as his wife's umbrella finally fell apart. He thrust the sheaf of papers at the cowering farmer.

"Read these," he ordered. "There's an

100

injunction forbidding you or anyone else to interfere with this pond till the Department of the Environment gives permission, which will be never. And there's some stuff about the barn, which is of historical interest and must on no account be altered in any way." Reuben stared in stunned disbelief at the documents in his clawlike hands, then sank to his knees and wept with vexation.

Prunella, shocked by Kenneth's antics with the shotgun and stunned by the abrupt appearance of his mother, stood gaping as Ada marched up to her.

"You look like an intelligent woman," Ada rapped. "It seems incredible to me that you seriously intend marrying someone who's been brought up from infancy to believe it's perfectly all right for a man to beat his wife."

"I – I had no idea," stammered Prunella. "I mean, you never really know someone till you live with them, do you?"

"Listen," hissed Ada. "I lived with his father long enough to know this: a Kilchaffinch is a Kilchaffinch. They're all the same and they never change. Marry my son and he'll make a skivvy of you." She shook her head. "Go, my dear. Leave while you've still got your freedom."

"Mum—!" Kenneth protested, but Prunella nodded.

"Yes. Yes, I think I will. I've been uncertain anyway – various things." She smiled wanly. "Thank you." She glanced at her former fiancé. "I'm sorry, Kenneth. So sorry."

She turned and began walking back towards the field gate. Kenneth shot his mother a murderous glance and started after her, but at that moment there was movement down by the gate. A Friesian cow came wandering into the field, followed by another, and then a third. The librarian skidded to a halt, turned, and ran in the opposite direction with the cheers of The Outfit ringing in his ears.

Professor Nichols picked up the shotgun, broke it, extracted the two cartridges and threw the empty weapon towards the snivelling Reuben. By the time he approached the children, he was smiling.

"I take it you're the people who wrote to me?"

Mickey nodded.

"I thought so. Well, I don't need to tell

you that you've done a splendid job. This pond isn't just one of your favourite places – it's a tremendously important part of the environment and it would have been a tragedy if it had been destroyed." He beamed. "You have averted two tragedies today."

Titch looked at him. "Two?"

The Professor nodded.

"Oh, yes. It would certainly have been a tragedy if that bright young woman had got hitched up to poor Kenneth." He smiled. "Ask my wife."

"Ask me what?" smiled Ada, coming across.

Mickey grinned. "We could all chat over a cup of tea," he suggested, "if you don't mind waiting till we get the stove going."

The couple said they didn't mind a bit, so Mickey called Raider to heel and they all trooped towards Weeping Wood. As they passed close to Reuben he looked up.

"You brats – you've ruined everything," he growled. Titch looked down at him.

"We didn't mean to," she cooed. "Honest."

CHAPTER 24

PERFECT END

"So what is it you've got to show us, Jillo?"

"Come in, sit down and you'll find out. Is Shaz on his way?"

Mickey nodded. He went down the library. He'll be here any minute."

"We'll wait for him, then."

"Tell you what," said Titch, "it doesn't seem like three weeks since all that fun by Froglet Pond, does it?"

Mickey shook his head. "No, Titch, it doesn't, but it is. Only one more week and we're back at school."

Jillo nodded. "I know, but who cares? It's been a fantastic holiday – especially for us." She grinned. "Froglet Pond's saved, Kenneth's left Lenton and the new librarian's terrific."

"And my dad's home," laughed Mickey.

"Who could ask for more?"

"But there is more," said Titch. "Wait and see."

"Wait and see what?" asked Shaz, sticking his head round the door.

"This," said Jillo dramatically. She produced a loosely wrapped parcel and placed it on the table.

"What's that?" demanded Mickey.

"Parcel," said Titch.

"Well, I know that. What's in it?"

"Da-daaa!" Jillo whipped away the brown paper to reveal a state-of-the-art MP3 player. The boys gazed at it.

"Wow!" breathed Shaz. "It's a real beauty, Jillo. Who got it for you?"

Jillo smiled. "Nobody got it for me," she said. "It's for us. It came with a card. Look." She passed a picture postcard across the table. The picture showed two great crested newts.

Mickey turned it over and read aloud:

"We thought this might come in handy at Outfit HQ. Thanks for the tea! Love Ada & Toby Nichols."

Shaz shook his head and grinned. "The perfect end to a perfect adventure," he said. "What d'you say we do the oath?"

And they did.

READ ALL OF THE OUTFIT'S THRILLING ADVENTURES!

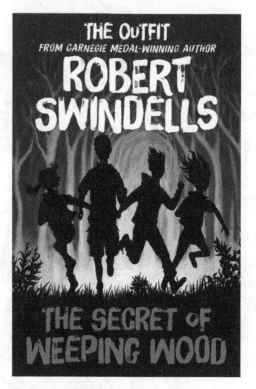

ISBN 978-1-78270-053-1

The Outfit had never really believed
the stories about the ghosts of Weeping
Wood – until now. But as they investigate
the mysterious cries, truth suddenly
becomes stranger – and more
terrifying – than fiction!

READ ALL OF THE OUTFIT'S THRILLING ADVENTURES!

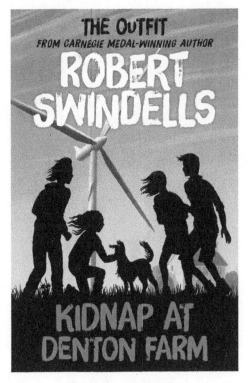

ISBN 978-1-78270-055-5

When Farmer Denton has a wind turbine
built on his farm, little does he know what
trouble it will bring. After one of them goes
missing, The Outfit must solve the mystery of
the malicious caller – and fast – if they ever
want to see their friend again!

READ ALL OF THE OUTFIT'S THRILLING ADVENTURES!

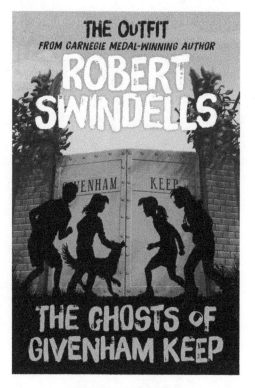

ISBN 978-1-78270-056-2

Steel gates and barbed wire have
been put up around the old mansion in
Weeping Wood. Someone has something to
hide and The Outfit intend to find out what.
But their innocent investigation soon
takes a sinister turn...

READ ALL OF THE OUTFIT'S THRILLING ADVENTURES!

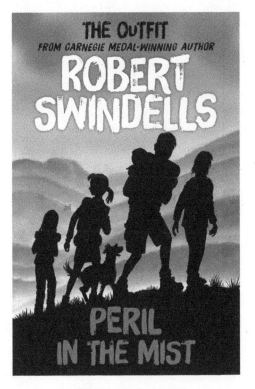

ISBN 978-1-78270-057-9

A challenging hike across five remote moors
is just the sort of adventure The Outfit love.
But when they find themselves alone on the
moors as mist descends and night falls,
will The Outfit be able to overcome
their greatest challenge yet?

READ ALL OF THE OUTFIT'S THRILLING ADVENTURES!

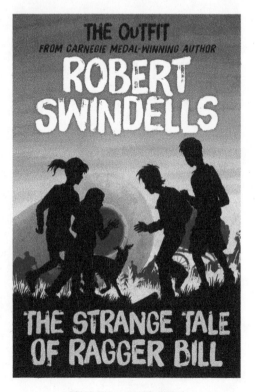

THE OUTFIT
FROM CARNEGIE MEDAL-WINNING AUTHOR
ROBERT SWINDELLS
THE STRANGE TALE OF RAGGER BILL

ISBN 978-1-78270-058-6

A little girl has gone missing and some of the villagers are taking matters into their own hands. Ragger Bill is the main suspect, but The Outfit are sure he is innocent. They must find the true culprit – and fast – before things go too far!